The Mosque
of Córdoba
Told
To Children

TEXT
Mª Dolores Baena Alcántara
Mª Teresa Baena Alcántara

DESIGNS
Pilarín Bayés de Luna

ENGLISH VERSION
Carolina Román Fernández and James Justin Daniell

EDICIONES MIGUEL SÁNCHEZ

© Ediciones Miguel Sánchez C.B.

C/ Marqués de Mondéjar, 44. Granada

© Dibujos: Bitono (paqui robles)

Impresión: Gráficas La Madraza

I.S.B.N.: 84-7169-063-2
Legal Deposit: GR-456-2001
Printed in Spain

The big day has come. Our friends, Teresa, Alvaro and Jorge are getting ready to visit the most important monument in their town, the Mezquita or Great Mosque in Córdoba. Jorge, who is really curious about these things, is anxious to know more details of this magnificent building which he passes every day on his way to school. Alvaro, eyes and ears wide open wants to understand all the stories, dates and curious facts so that he can tell the group of foreign students who are coming on an exchange. Teresa, notebook in hand, cannot wait to start asking questions and jotting things down. Come along and join us on this visit and we´ll have a real adventure!

A BIT OF HISTORY

Once upon a time there was, and still is, a city in the south of Spain called Córdoba. It is one of the oldest towns in Spain and is located on the banks of the river Guadalquivir, which runs through eastern Andalusia. Córdoba has always been a special place because it is situated at a crossroads in the middle of Andalusia.

Throughout the centuries, many people of different origins, religions and cultures have lived together there helping create its rich history and tradition.

Let´s start by saying that Spain has been visited and invaded by many foreign peoples. The Phoenicians and the Greeks came to trade; the Carthaginians continued trading and stayed here for many years; the Romans made Córdoba the capital of their kingdom, which they called *Bética*, a territory which corresponds to what we now know as Andalusia; then came the Visigoths, who remained in the town until the arrival of the Arab forces. From all these people we have inherited words, customs, architecture and art.

Arabs, also called Muslims or Moors, came to Córdoba in the year 715 AD. They came from a kingdom across the Mediterranean Sea, conquering most of northern Africa and then moved into Spain. The area of Spain conquered by the Moorish troops was named **Al-Andalus**, and this is where the word *Andalusia* comes from.

In the middle of the 8th century, an Arab king known as Abd al-Rahman I established a state known as the Independent Emirat. He was the first member of the famous Arab dynasty of the Umayyad and ruled over *Al-Andalus* until the 11th century.

Abd al-Rahman III established a new system of government called the Caliphate

and named himself *Califa* an Arab word which means "prince of the believers". During this period, Córdoba became one of the most important cities in the world. At this time the central part of the city was the Medina, or walled city, where you could find the main mosque, the Alcázar (the residence of the Califa and his court) *zocos* (souks) and *alcaicerías* (a kind of market), public baths, and many other mosques.

This prosperous period under the Caliphate ended in the 11th century due to fights among the Arabs themselves, and then the Al-Andalus region split up into small independent kingdoms called *taifas*. Afterwards, two tribes from northern Africa took control: the Almoravids and the Almohads. But the Christians from the north of Spain were ready to make the most of the recent divisions and re-took some of the Arab territory, reaching Córdoba in the year 1236 under the orders of the Catholic King Ferdinand III.

Today in Córdoba there are many signs of the old Arab civilization together with elements from other cultures. In fact, Córdoba is known as the town of the three cultures: Arab, Jewish and Christian, all of whom lived there together during the Middle Ages.

A WALK AROUND THE GREAT MOSQUE

Before entering the Great Mosque, our friends Alvaro, Teresa and Jorge, together with Felipe, Alvaro and Teresa´s father, decide to go for a walk. Let´s join them on their way around the *Juderia*, or Jewish quarter. We go in through **Almodóvar´s Gate**, part of the wall which surrounded the *Medina*.

Some signs of the different cultures which are present in the town are: the **Caliphal Baths of the Alcázar** (the King´s palace) from the 10th century, situated in the gardens known as *"Campo Santo de los Mártires"* (Holy field of the marthyrs); the **Alcázar of the Christian Kings** built in the 14thcentury, and the **Synagogue**, the place where Jewish people used to meet to worship or to study their religion.

Another famous characteristic of the city are the famous *patios*. Of extreme beauty, their fountains, plants and trees bring down the temperature in the hot summer days and become the centre of a famous May Festival.

Our friends now make their way to the **Puerta del Puente**, erected in the 16th century. While looking at the Roman bridge or **Puente**, Alvaro comes across the great **Tower of Calahorra**, built in the 14th century over the remains of another Arab tower. Once on the bridge, the group look at the Arabic **Mill of the Albolafia**, with its superb waterwheel. This is an opportunity for Jorge to show off by remarking: "Did you know that this wheel can be seen in the emblem of the town?"

What a lovely walk! But it is time for our friends to go into the Great Mosque, where we will have another opportunity to see the mixture of cultures found throughout the town.

"How can so many different influences be found in a single building?" asked Teresa in amazement. "Well, this is because it started as an Arab mosque and then the Christians built a Cathedral inside it after conquering the town" answered Alvaro.

THE GREAT MOSQUE AND ITS ENLARGEMENTS

Let´s start by getting some information about it. Our little friends already know that a mosque is the building where Muslims go to worship. Their religion is Islam, taught by the prophet Mohammed. Muslims believe that there is one god, Allah and their 'bible' or sacred book is known as the Koran. Mosques are made up of two main areas: the *sanh* or **patio** with a **tower** (*alminar*) and the masŷid or indoor **praying room**.

Is that all ? Of course not! It is worth knowing in fact that the Mosque had to be enlarged on several different occasions to come to be as it is today. A first mosque was built by Abd al-Rahman I in the 8th century and then three extensions were carried out in the 9th and 10th centuries by the Arab kings Abd Al-Rahman II, Al-Hakam II and Al-Mansur. Finally, in the 16th century a Christian cathedral was built inside.

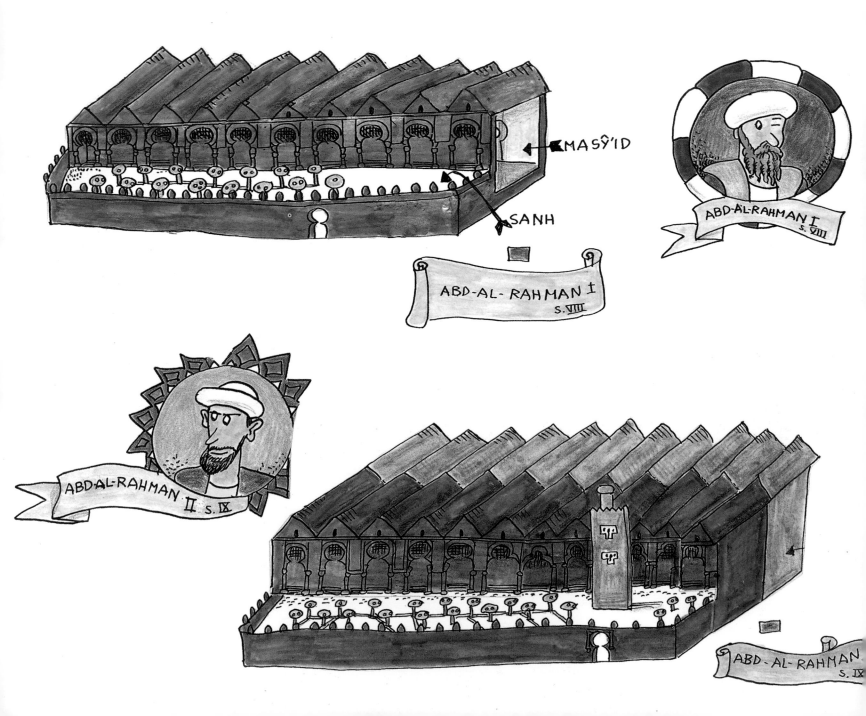

AL-HAKAM II
S. X

AL
HAKAM
II
S. X

ALMANZOR
S. X

ALMANZOR
S. X

ALONSO MANRIQUE

REFORMA CRISTIANA S. XVI

Plan and view of the Mosque nowadays after all the extensions and the construction of the Christian Cathedral

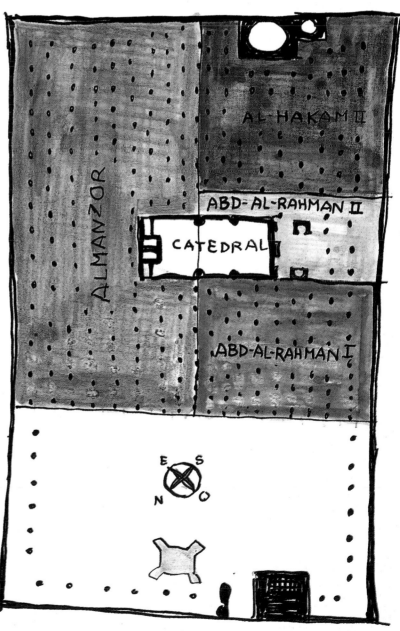

AL-HAKAM II

ABD-AL-RAHMAN II

ALMANZOR

CATEDRAL

ABD-AL-RAHMAN I

THE GREAT MOSQUE AND THE COURTYARD OF THE ORANGE TREES

From the outside, the Great Mosque looks like a fortress riddled with doors. Jorge, Teresa and Alvaro get into the Mosque by the main door called **The Gate of Forgiveness** *(Puerta del Perdón)*. Do you know where the name comes from? It was the place where repentant christians used to go to be publicly forgiven for their sins.

Through this gate we enter the **Patio de los Naranjos** or **Courtyard of the Orange trees**. It is great fun to go and drink from the four water spouts at the fountain! An elderly man sitting quietly in the court tells them about a very peculiar old saying: "Do you know, my little friends," he says, "that whoever drinks from the spout under the olive tree is sure to get married?" How funny! This courtyard is a wonderful place to walk, read or talk quietly…and this is precisely what locals and tourists often do.

While messing around in the courtyard, our friends are surprised by a ditch near the door of the praying room (the indoor area of the

Mosque). As they approach, they find a group of men and women carefully excavating a wall. Curious, the children ask one of the women what she is drawing on a piece of paper. She is an archaelogist!

She is called Marta and tells them that this is an archaelogical excavation. They are trying to discover the remains under the Mosque to know what was there before. They are also investigating how the Mosque was built. "Wow! It`s like a detective story where you

have to find clues, solve the mystery and discover how history itself unfolded!" cry our friends.

Teresa takes the opportunity to ask Marta a few questions and jot down the answers in her notebook. "Now the foreign students will get all the details," she states. "What was here before?" asks Teresa.

According to Marta, this is called the **Mezquita "Aljama"**, which means "the most important one," as there were many others scattered around the town. It is one of the finest examples of Arab architecture. The Muslims used to go there on the most important day of their week, Friday, to pray. However, only men were allowed into the building and women had to remain outside.

Before that, in its place was a Visigothic Church called the *Basílica de San Vicente.* In the year 751 A.D., the Arab King Abd al-Rahman I reached an agreement with the Visigoths (who were

Christians) and bought part of the Church to make a place where the Muslims could pray, and so it became a place where both Muslims and Christians worshipped their Gods.

"And who was Abd al-Rahman?" Jorge asks. "He was one of the members of the famous Umayyad family who came from Syria to Spain," answers Alvaro.

And he is quite right. Abd al-Rahman was the first Emir (Muslim ruler) of al-Andalus, and he was known as "The Fair". He was said to be a tall, fair-haired man with one eye. He was a warrior, but also a poet and a good public speaker.

Soon the area bought from the Christians was too small for the growing number of Muslims in the town and therefore, between the years 780

and 785 Abd al-Rahman decided to buy the rest of the Church of St. Vincent and build a mosque. We know this because excavations have brought to light remains of the old church. There are also signs of the Christian church in the columns and supports we can now find in the Arab building.

But this mosque built by "The Fair" is only one part of the Great Mosque. During the 9th and 10th centuries the building was enlarged to host the growing number of citizens in the town.

Next to the Mosque, there were two other halls known as the *ablution halls*. Ablution means washing yourself and in these halls the Muslim worshipers washed themselves to "purify" their bodies before praying. On the Eastern side of the Mosque across the street, archaeologists have found the ablution hall of Al-Mansur, the last Muslim ruler to enlarge the building.

THE ALMINAR OR TOWER.- Let's continue with some more history. As the prayer room got bigger and bigger, so did the Courtyard of the Orange Trees. The son of Abd al-Rahman, Hixam I, built the first alminar, a slender tower connected to the mosque, which was pulled down some years later to make the Courtyard bigger.

The tallest **alminar** found in the Great Mosque was built in the 10th century by Abd al-Rahman III. He was the first Caliph or ruler of *Al-Andalus*. He created a magnificent court where philosophy, arts, poetry and history blossomed, turning Córdoba not only into a political and economic centre but also one of the greatest cultural centres in the world.

When you go up to the top of the tower, it is odd to see that the walls and steps are different. How is this possible? Well, because in the 17th-century the **Cathedral Tower** was built around the alminar, covering it. Finally, all the climbing is rewarded when you see many bells at the top of the tower, including the "huge cathedral bell".

It was from there, at the top of the tower, where the muezzin, the official of the mosque, used to call the Muslims to prayer. Our friends know all about this because every midday they can hear to the muezzin from a nearby mosque. Isn´t that amazing?

The group say goodbye to the archaeologist and go into the prayer room, the indoor part of The Great Mosque. They enter through the **Puerta de las Palmas or Palm Gate**, which takes its name from the Christian celebrations on Palm Sunday.

The **first mosque** which was built by Abd al-Rahman I consisted of 11 naves ending at a great wall called a **qibla**. The qibla is the wall found in all mosques which points to Mecca, the holiest city in Islam to which Muslims must turn when praying. However, it is curious that in Córdoba, due to its construction over what had been houses, the qibla points slightly to the south of Mecca.

The building is supported by a system of **arches and columns** instead of using traditional walls. The aisles are separated at the top by walls leaning on columns which are in turn held by arches forming endless arcades. Architects used horseshoe arches on the lower parts and semicircular ones on the upper parts.

"How big it is and how many arches!" "It looks like a column forest!", exclaims Teresa at the sight of the building.

THE CONSTRUCTION OF THE GREAT MOSQUE

After all we have seen from the courtyard and its surroundings, it seems that the building is "alive". Here, for centuries different cultures have worked and prayed and now many people still work here to keep up its splendour.

Walking around the endless rows of columns, we meet Mercedes. She is an architect and she is studying how the Mosque was built. She says that knowing the building better can help us preserve this beautiful place. Did you know that architects not only build houses, but also restore and preserve old buildings? One of the children asks: "Why are there so many arches?" "Well," she says, "Would you like to hear the story of how this forest of columns was built?"

This is a revolutionary system which allowed for a taller building with a roof held in such a original way that all the aisles can be seen at the same time. It worked so well that soon many other buildings followed this design.

However, this is not just an Arab "invention". Architects took the idea from the arches which supported Roman aqueducts carrying water supplies to cities and from the horseshoe arches in Visigothic buildings.

This side of the First Mosque looks like a museum, full of many different **columns and supports**. "And do you know why?" asks Mercedes.

"Yes I do," answers Jorge. "It`s because they used old pieces from the old Visigothic church, like a kind of recycling".

"Exactly, Jorge," says the architect, "but the recycling process also includes Roman remains. The Muslims saved a lot materials in this building".

"And what kind of paint is there on the arches?", asks Alvaro, "They aren`t painted, although they seem to be. Each arch is made up of wedge-shaped stones called **voussoirs**: the red ones are made of brick whereas the yellow ones are of limestone".

Look! Over there there is a kind of ramp on the floor. It is the place where the first qibla wall was located. It was pulled down by Abd al-Rahman II to enlarge the Mosque. This was the **first enlargement** where re-used materials began to be mixed with new ones. Abd al-Rahman II, like other members of the Umayyad families, encouraged the arts and sciences, along with agriculture and industry. He was a poet and brought into Europe a new taste for oriental culture and luxury. He brought the most famous wise men and artists to his court, such as the musician Ziryab, and, among other things, is resposible for making chess become the popular game we currently enjoy!

The taste for luxury, however, has nothing to do with the marble floor we are walking on, as it is not the original one. The original floor of the Great Mosque was made of hard, pressed soil, probably mixed with a special kind of red clay known as *almagra* and covered with an endless number of carpets or rugs, as you can still see in mosques all over the world.

The son of Abd al-Rahman III, Al-Hakam II performed the **second enlargement** of the prayer room on the Guadalquivir river side. There are no "recycled" columns or supports here, as they were specially designed for this purpose. This is the most elaborately decorated area, and served as a proof of the importance and riches of

the second Caliph. Al-Hakam was the ruler who gave most importance to culture in Al-Andalus. He had a vast library, very famous in its time, where he had a workshop for drawing miniatures, binding and copying books (as you probably know, at this time there was no printing system, so books had to be hand-written). He surrounded himself with wise men, artists and writers and created free schools for children in Córdoba and one of the most famous universities of the day.

At the end of the room, there is an area separated from the rest by a gate. At the front next to the qibla there is a small room decorated in marble called the **mihrab**: this is the place showing in

which direction Muslims must face to pray. In front of the worshippers, a holy man would read from the Koran.

In front of the mihrab, we find the **maqsura**, which is like a royal box, where the court of the Caliph would

stand. It was separated from the rest by a wooden banister which is now made of iron.

On this side of the qibla, the arches of the doors are decorated in a way which reminds you of the Roman mosaics you can see at the Archaelogical Museum. And indeed, they are **mosaics** in a Roman style, brought across the Mediterranean sea as a gift from the Emperor of Byzantium to the Caliph of Córdoba. The difference was that the Romans used these mosaics to decorate the floor whereas in Byzantium they were used on the walls.

The ceiling over the maqsura has a different decoration: it is made up of crossed arches, decorated with pieces of carved stone and marble known as *atauriques*. The open windows at the top or *lucernarios* (ventilating ridge tiles) brought light into the building, which had become dark after so many extensions. There were also many **chandeliers** hanging from the ceiling lit by oil lamps different from those you can see nowadays.

ATAURIQUES

The third and final enlargement could not be carried out on the riverside, and so it was performed on the Eastern side. During the rule of Al-Mansur in the year 987, eight new aisles were added and the courtyard was also enlarged resulting in the patio which exists today. In contrast to the other areas, the arches here are painted, as they were not made of brick but of stone. Al-Mansur, also known as "The Victorious" was the first minister of the Caliph Hixem II. He was a famous warrior well known for his raids into the Christian kingdoms. He had reached as far as Santiago, in northern Spain, and brought back to Córdoba the bells of Santiago´s church as a part of the war loot.

The writings from that time say that, in order to enlarge the building, Al-Mansur intended to build over a street and its houses. However, not all the owners wanted to sell their houses. In fact, there was an old lady who did not want to leave her house with its patio and beautiful orange tree and Al-Mansur was forced to build a new house exactly the same as the old one for the lady and plant the orange tree there. This seems to be true, as archaeologists have uncovered this street during their excavations.

This is all I can tell you about the construction of the Arab building. Now you can look for Paco, an Art historian who also works in the conservation of the Mosque.

The children continue their visit and get to the central area of the building where they meet Paco. He is studying all the elements of the building, separating the different parts and the specific decoration in each of them. This is very important, as this information will help him maintain and restore any areas in a bad state of repair. Once Paco finds out about the children´s interest in the Mosque, he offers to show them the Cathedral area.

"How lucky we are," says Teresa

"Very much so", answers Jorge, "They are giving us all the information we need to know about this amazing building".

THE CATHEDRAL AND THE CHRISTIAN REFORMATIONS

After all the enlargements made by the Arabs, the building underwent another series of reformations. The most significant of these was the building of the Cathedral between the 16th and 18th centuries.

But let´s see some other changes first. After Ferdinand III and Isabella, the Catholic Kings, re-conquered the town in 1236, the Great Mosque became a Christian Church, and it was named Sta. María la Mayor. Some time later, at the end of the ailes built by Al-Mansur, the Chapel of St. Clement was built and here mass was celebrated until 1257, an area belonging to the enlargement made by Al-Hakam II was made into the **Villaviciosa Chapel**. On one side of the chapel there is a big room, beautifully decorated with carvings on the walls. This is the **Royal Chapel**, built by the Spanish King Henry II as a burial place for some of the Kings. The decoration in the chapel is of Arabic style, as it was crafted by Muslim artists still living in Spain after the Christian reconquest of the town. This special Arab style in Christian buildings is known as **mudéjar**.

Walking across the Villaviciosa Chapel you can find some large pointed arches, quite different from the horseshoe and semicircular ones seen in the Mosque. They set the limits of the aisle which forms the **First Cathedral**, built in a **Gothic style** of architecture. Gothic architecture was commonly found in Western Europe in the Middle Ages. Gothic cathedrals are really high, as if they wanted to reach the sky.

In the 16th century, a bishop called Alonso Manrique considered that the Main Chapel and the Choir should not be placed along one side of the Mosque. Therefore, he decided to build what we now know as the **Cathedral** in the middle of it, pulling down most of the work done by Abd al-Rahman II and some of that done by Al-Mansur.

LOS REYES CATOLICOS

DOÑA ISABEL DON FERNANDO

However, the citizens of the town did not like the idea. They knew that this was a special building, unique in its kind and that these reformations would partially destroy it. Therefore, the Town Council decided not to build the cathedral. They made a public announcement telling bricklayers, stonemasons and carpenters not to work in the church. If any of them were to break this rule, they would pay with their lives. These differences between the Church and the Town Coucil about whether or not to build the cathedral were taken to the emperor himself, Charles I. The emperor was on the side of the archbishop and the cathedral was built. Some time later, after visiting the Mosque and seeing the building works of the cathedral, Carlos realized how foolish he had been and exclaimed:

"If I had known this, I would not have let it touch the old building. You have built what you or others might have built anywhere, but you have destroyed something that was unique in the world"

He then understood the claims of the Town Council. There were churches like this in other places, but there was not other place in the world like the Great Mosque. But it was too late: the works were well under way.

"At least the vast majority of the Arab building still remains," said Alvaro.

This is the reason, my little friends, why the Cathedral has become an unusual work, as they erected one building within another.

The Cathedral is cross-shaped and this is why the central area is known as the crossing or transept. The works for the **Main Chapel and the Transept** started in they year 1523 under the direction of Hernán Ruiz, *el Viejo* (The Old) and were continued by his son and grandson. They were a famous family of architects, also responsible for other buildings considered as masterpieces representative of the Renaissance style, an artistic style which came after the Gothic and imitated Roman trends.

However, while the cathedral was being built between the 16th and 18th centuries, it became a

mixture of different decorations and art styles: you can find examples as well as elements from **Renaissance and Baroque styles**. The Baroque style emerged during the 17th and 18th centuries and is characterized by elaborate decoration.

The **Main Altarpiece**, made of red marble, and the **Choir Stalls** are both worthy of note. The choir stalls are one of the most important works in the cathedral, made up of lines of chairs where the canons or members of the clergy sit. Among these chairs there is one which looks like a throne: it is the chair of the bishop and is known as the "cátedra" and this is the origin of the word "cathedral".

The choir stalls are carved of mahogany, a material of great quality brought from the island of Cuba by the tall ships which traded with the Americas. The choir stalls are decorated with stories and figures from the Bible, the sacred book of the Christians.

The pulpits are also made of carved wood. You know what? There is an old saying about the figure of an ox carved on the pulpit. People say that it represents one of the oxen which carried the stones used to make the pulpit. They say it died of exhaustion due to the strenuous work. But that is just an old saying, because what the ox represents really is one of the symbols of the biblical gospel writers, like all the other figures found there.

Another Christian reformation in the Great Mosque was the introduction of over fifty Chapels attached to its walls. Most of them were built during the Renaissance and Baroque periods. Many of them are burial places, like the one devoted to the famous Spanish writer Luis de Góngora.

Do you want to know about another old saying? Look at the chapel which has a cross carved on the column. People say that the cross was carved by a Christian prisoner using his nails. Next to it, there is a wax statue which was supposed to cry whenever a flame was brought near it. In fact, there are many stories about Christians being made prisoners in the Mosque, but they are simply tales, as we all know that people could never have been made prisoners inside a sacred place!

CESAR ARBASSIA ME FECIT S. XVI

Let's now move to the **Capilla del Sagrario** which is situated at the end of the Mosque. It takes up three aisles and is completely covered with paintings. Well, I am afraid I will have to leave you now, I must go back to work.

What a coincidence! In this Chapel the children meet Pedro, a restorer. Pedro is now cleaning and restoring those paintings in bad condition and preventing others from getting damaged.

"What are those paintings all over the walls?" asks Teresa.

They are paintings made using a technique known as *fresco*. They were painted on the fresh lime and sand of the wall. The wall is first rough-plastered and then a coat is applied so that the paint sticks better to the walls. This kind of decoration was used in the 16th century by an Italian Rainassance painter known as Cesar Arbasia.

In the Cathedral and Christian Chapels you can also find many other works of art. There are many paintings and sculpures by important artists. Did

you know that in the Cathedral you can also find **Treasure**? It is exhibited in two rooms of the Barroque Chapel of Cardenal Salazar. Also of great interest is the collection of typical silverware from Córdoba. The town has been famous for its silversmiths for centuries. The most important example of this is the **Custodia Procesional** or monstrance, which is taken on a procession through the streets during the religious festival of Corpus Christi. It is huge and was crafted in silver and gold by Enrique de Arfe in the 16th century.

"Wow! Many artists from different places came to work in the Mosque and in the Cathedral!" Jorge comments.

"Yes," said Alvaro "and with so many artworks you must have lots to do, Pedro."

"That`s right. But I do not only work with Christian pictures and sculptures. We also have to take care not only of the Islamic paintings and decorations but also of the painted wooden beams on the ceiling of the Mosque. And restoration is a long and painstaking process, as we have to be very careful with the art works. I hope I have been helpful."

"Of course. Thank you very much Pedro!" exclaim the three children.

This is the end of our adventure. The children say goodbye and thank everybody for helping them to understand the story of the Great

FERNANDEZ DE ANGULO

DAMIAN DE CASTRO

ENRIQUE PEARCE

Mosque. As you can see, many professionals work together for a common goal: to know more in order to preserve and to preserve in order to help us know more.

"What a great amount of information to share with our exchange students!" says Alvaro with excitement.

"I hope that you wrote down some of the information, Teresa," Jorge remarks.

"Of course I did and now I know both how important the Mosque is, and why we must help preserve it: so that other children can enjoy it in the future," answers Teresa.

Felipe, the children´s father, who has been with them during the whole visit, remarks: "Not only children, but everybody should think about what you´ve just said, Teresa".

And they all decide to come back again and learn more about this stunning monument.

We hope you will want to come back too...